This Walker book belongs to:

- - - - - - - - -

- - - - - - - - -

Moo
Moo
Say Hello
Like This!
Mary Murphy

A dog hello
is licky
and loud ...

A cat hello is

prissy
and proud ...

A frog hello
is jumpy
and croaky ...

A chicken hello
is flappy

and clucky...

A beetle hello

is tiny
and
tappy ...

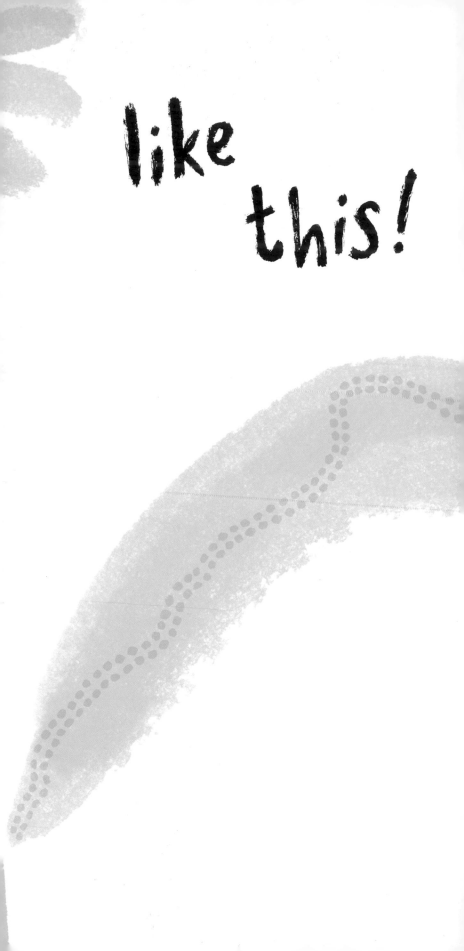

like
this!

tip
tap tip tip tip
tip tap tap tip tip tap
tip tap tip tap
tap tip tap tap
tip tap tip tap
tip tap
tap tip tap
tip tap
tap tip tap
tap tip
tap

tap
tip tip
tip tap tap
tip tip
tap
tip

A donkey
silly and

hello is

happy ...

Other books by Mary Murphy:

978-1-4063-3908-6

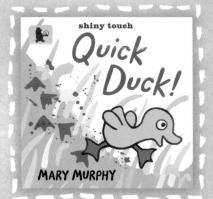

978-1-4063-3907-9

978-1-4063-4828-6

978-1-4063-2996-4

978-1-4063-4538-4

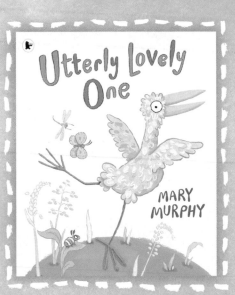

978-1-4063-3774-7

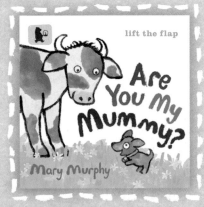

978-1-4063-5378-5

Available from all good booksellers

www.walker.co.uk